MAIRI'S MOTORBIKE

Contents

Written by Lynne Rickards

Illustrated by Eugene Smith

Collins

1 EARLY YEARS

Mairi Chisholm was born on 26th February 1896. In her school graduation photo, she looked prim and proper, like most other young girls in those days. But hidden behind that gentle appearance was a lively and energetic spirit longing for adventure and freedom.

Mairi loved motorbikes. Her older brother had a fast one, and he was a keen racer. She watched him speed around the track, spraying clouds of dust. It was so exciting! Mairi loved the roar of the engines. She imagined how thrilling it would be to feel the wind in her face as she crossed the finish line. She would leave them all behind! Mairi Chisholm the champion! It was all she could think about.

Mairi asked her mum and dad if she could have a motorbike. She was sure she could win a race too.

Her big brother agreed. He knew she could do anything she set her mind to. Mairi's parents were surprised. A teenage girl ride a motorbike? It was almost unheard of. In 1913, girls wore ankle-length skirts and high-necked blouses. How would she even get on to a motorbike, let alone ride it?

Whin Croft, Mairi's home in Dorset

School was finished, and Mairi was home for the summer.
Her family was very wealthy and they lived in a big house with
lots of land. At 17, she was expected to play tennis with her
rich friends, dress up and go to dances where she would find
a husband. But Mairi hated all that "girly" stuff. She didn't
want to get married! Not now, anyway.

She was much happier dressed in her brother's old clothes,
helping him fix his motorbikes in the stables. That summer,
he competed in a few local races, and Mairi went along as
his mechanic. She was very good at it too! A female mechanic
was a rare thing, so people started to notice. One friend of her
parents was so impressed, he told them she should have her
own motorbike.

Mairi's mum wouldn't hear of it. She thought all this boyish behaviour would ruin her daughter. In her opinion, proper young ladies did not ride motorbikes. Mairi would have messy hair and always be greasy with motor oil. What would people say?

Mairi didn't care about that. She didn't want to be a proper young lady. They never had any fun. She didn't care what anyone said, either. It really felt very unfair.

Mairi's dad was proud of her skills as a mechanic. He didn't
say anything, but he was listening to what she said.
On one hand, he could see that motorbike racing was dirty
and dangerous. On the other hand, if he let his son have
a motorbike, then why not his daughter? Mairi had made
a good point. It wasn't fair. He thought about it a while longer.
Then he went to his study and picked up the telephone.

A few days later, a shiny new Douglas motorbike arrived at the house. It was long and low with a black frame and sturdy tyres. Mairi sat on the front steps looking annoyed. Another bike for her brother? How many did he need?

But to Mairi's amazement, this motorbike was for her! As her dad pointed out, it was only fair.

Mairi couldn't believe her ears. Her very own motorbike at last! Her greatest wish had come true!

2 MAD MOTORCYCLE DAYS

That autumn, Mairi spent as much time as she could in a pair of her brother's old overalls, riding around the stable yard on her new motorbike. It didn't take long before she was a skilled rider. She already knew how to keep her bike running smoothly. She could strip down the engine and repair it like a professional. She could fix a flat tyre in a flash.

Her mother was still horrified, and pointed out that she'd been right. It was true – Mairi did have wild hair and was always covered in motor oil. But did she care? Not one bit.

Mairi started riding around the grounds of her family home in Dorset. Next, she ventured out on to the local lanes where she could go a bit faster.

It wasn't long before Mairi was a motorcycle ace roaring around the country roads of Dorset and Hampshire with the wind in her face. It was all just as thrilling as she'd imagined!

Later that autumn, Mairi came across an amazing woman riding her own motorbike with a **sidecar**. She wore a long leather coat with her dark hair swept up into a stylish cap. Mairi couldn't believe it! Here was another free spirit who loved the open road, just like her! Mairi rushed over and introduced herself.

The lady motorcyclist was pleased to meet Mairi. Her name was Mrs Elsie Knocker, but people called her "Gypsy" because she was always on the move, and she belonged to the Gypsy Motor Cycle Club.

Mairi and Elsie had a lot in common. They were both quite unusual, being lady motorcyclists. They were both expert mechanics who didn't mind getting dirty. They both loved speed and danger. The only difference was their age, as Elsie was more than ten years older than Mairi.

Soon, Mairi and Elsie were best friends, zooming around the country lanes together. They entered motorbike and sidecar trials, competing as a team. As the months passed, their friendship grew. In the summer of 1914, Mairi and Elsie were looking forward to a 193 kilometre motorcycle trial they had signed up for in the middle of August. But on 4th August, everything changed forever. It was the day Britain declared war on Germany.

Elsie and her bike

GREAT BRITAIN DECLARES WAR ON GERMANY.

SUMMARY REJECTION OF BRITISH ULTIMATUM.

The following announcement was issued at the Foreign Office at 12.15 a.m. :—

"Owing to the summary rejection by the German Government of the request made by His Majesty's Government for assurances that the neutrality of Belgium would be respected, His Majesty's Ambassador in Berlin has received his passports, and His Majesty's Government has declared to the German Government that a state of war exists between Great Britain and Germany as from 11 p.m. on August 4."

Huge crowds in Whitehall and Trafalgar Square greeted the news with round after round of cheers.

11 p.m. London time is midnight Berlin time, the hour at which the British ultimatum expired.

3 BRITAIN DECLARES WAR!

Young men across the country were volunteering to fight. German troops had invaded Belgium and they had to be stopped!

Mairi and Elsie wanted to do something too. It seemed terrible to sit around doing nothing when the country was at war and people were suffering. Elsie thought they could drive their motorbikes to London and join the **Women's Emergency Corps.** The Corps had been set up to train women as doctors, nurses and motorcycle messengers. Mairi and Elsie's driving skills would be very useful. They were also expert mechanics, and Elsie had nursing training. Mairi jumped on the idea. It was perfect for them!

But Mairi was only 18. She needed her parents' permission.

Mairi's mum was not happy about the plan. She argued that proper young ladies shouldn't go racing around London on their own. Mairi insisted that she and Elsie wanted to do their bit. Mairi's dad was on her side. He thought it was brilliant that she wanted to help the war effort. Mairi's mum worried that she was far too young, but her dad was convinced that Mairi had a good head on her shoulders. He felt it would be a great experience for her. Mairi's mum still thought it was a crazy idea.

While her mum and dad were arguing, Mairi tiptoed upstairs. She quickly tied a change of underwear and some cash into a headscarf and sneaked down to the back door.

Her parents were still shouting as she slipped out, hopped on her motorbike and headed for Elsie's place. Nothing was going to stop her now, permission or no permission!

The next morning, Mairi and Elsie set off on their bikes. They didn't care what anyone said. Next stop, London! Mairi had never felt so free. She couldn't wait to be doing something useful!

Once they arrived in London, Mairi and Elsie signed up as **dispatch riders** with the Women's Emergency Corps.

They carried important messages and orders from Army Headquarters to military units around London. Soon they were whizzing back and forth across the city in busy traffic. They had to move fast. The success of army communications depended on them. It took a lot of skill and steady nerves. Mairi loved it!

4 FLYING AMBULANCE CORPS

A few weeks later, a doctor called Hector Munro was standing on a London street corner. He was on the lookout for skilled and fearless drivers to join his superfast **"Flying" Ambulance Corps** in Belgium.

Suddenly, Mairi flew past him doing a crazy hairpin turn on her motorbike through the traffic. He knew right away she would make a brilliant ambulance driver. He tracked her down at the Women's Emergency Corps and asked her to come to Belgium. Heavy fighting had broken out there and the German troops were gaining ground. Many Belgian soldiers and civilians were being killed and injured, and they needed help. Dr Munro's ambulance drivers would bring wounded soldiers from the battlefield to an army hospital. It was hard work, and very dangerous.

Dr Munro asked Mairi if she would join his team in Belgium. He hoped that she would take the job. Mairi thought it would be an adventure. "Yes, I'd love to," she replied, without hesitation.

But Mairi couldn't leave Elsie behind. She told her new boss that Elsie had excellent driving skills and training as a nurse, and she could speak French and German. Mairi was thrilled when Elsie joined Dr Munro's Flying Ambulance Corps as well.

In late September 1914, Mairi and Elsie travelled by boat to Belgium with Dr Munro and the ten other people he'd chosen from over 200 applicants. They included two doctors, two London bus drivers and three wealthy society ladies. The two bus drivers each brought a car on the journey, and Elsie had her Chater-Lea motorcycle and sidecar with her. It would be useful for carrying wounded soldiers off the muddy battlefields where a heavier car might get stuck. Mairi's beloved Douglas motorbike would be no use for helping the wounded, so she sold

it to pay her way in Belgium. She would be driving the other vehicles from now on. There was no turning back.

Elsie and Mairi in London

The seas were calm on the four-hour journey across
the Channel, and Dr Munro's group were excited about
their adventure! They sang silly **music hall** songs together,
laughed and chatted the whole way.

On arrival in Belgium, they spent one night in the port of
Ostend, then travelled east to Ghent.

Mairi's journey

Canterbury

Dover

ENGLAND

Ostend

Ghent

Dunkirk

BELGIUM

FRANCE

24

Mairi, who spent her holidays in the Scottish highlands, was amazed at how flat the Belgian landscape looked.

Not far from Ghent, the German invaders had bombed and burnt out towns and villages. Hundreds of Belgians were streaming along the roads to escape the fighting. Over 8,000 of these **refugees** were given shelter in Ghent. Mairi and Elsie spent their first few days helping to feed them all.

5 WORKING IN BELGIUM

Soon Mairi and Elsie felt impatient. They had come to Belgium to be ambulance drivers, and they wanted to get driving! But cars need petrol, and that was in short supply. It was so frustrating! With very little petrol, they couldn't make many trips to collect wounded soldiers during their first week. They passed their time in Ghent drinking tea, buying postcards and playing games with the soldiers in hospital.

Then, in early October, a series of trains from Antwerp brought in over 800 badly-wounded Belgian soldiers. Mairi was shocked at the sight of such terrible injuries, but there was a job to do.

She and Elsie worked hard all night giving first aid and transporting the men from the train station to hospital. They'd got some petrol at last, so the next night, Mairi went with a driver and two doctors to look for injured soldiers in the **trenches**. It was the first time she had been so close to the fighting.

Mairi saw the sky glowing red with burning buildings and heard the boom of German guns all around. They found one injured man and got him out on a stretcher. It took over two hours to drive him back to the hospital in Ghent on dark and dangerous roads. Mairi was exhausted, but happy to be finally working!

A few days later, on 7th October, Mairi's father arrived in Belgium. He had been sent by her mother with stern instructions to bring Mairi home!

Mairi showed him around Ghent, and at dinner she and Elsie told him stories of the terrible things they had seen. Soon Mairi was called away to drive wounded soldiers from several battle locations back to Ghent. Her father was very impressed, and a little bit jealous! He decided to go back to England without her. Mairi wrote his parting words to her in her diary:

"If it weren't for your mother I'd stay out here with you. You're having the most wonderful time. I wouldn't take you back for anything."

6 THE STRUGGLE TO SAVE LIVES

By mid-October, the fighting moved closer to Ghent and a new field hospital was set up further west in the town of Furnes. Dr Munro's Flying Ambulance Corps drove all their vehicles to Furnes and moved into an empty house.

Now Mairi and Elsie were working flat out rescuing soldiers from the front lines and helping in the new hospital. There were so many wounded that beds ran out, and some men had to be laid on stretchers on the floor. Mairi and Elsie made regular trips to the trenches after dark looking for soldiers needing help. Sometimes the only way Mairi could get a man out was to lift him on her back and carry him. They needed nerves of steel driving back to Furnes, as German bombs lit up the sky and **snipers'** bullets could hit them at any moment.

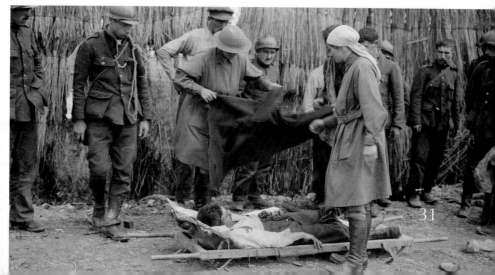

The road to the hospital was long and bumpy. Driving in the dark without headlights, it was difficult to avoid the bomb craters and other crashed vehicles along the way. Mairi and Elsie knew they had to move fast. The sooner the wounded men were treated, the better their chances of survival.

Mairi and Elsie rescued Belgian, French and even enemy German soldiers. In addition to their injuries, the men were already weakened from living for weeks in the trenches. Their clothes were wet and caked with mud. Their teeth chattered in the autumn chill. They suffered mentally too, from a lack of proper food or sleep, and from **shell shock** and fear. Mairi and Elsie worked hard to give them the best chance they could, but sometimes it wasn't enough.

7 LOOKING FOR A SOLUTION

In November, winter set in. Mairi and Elsie were tired
and discouraged. Too often on their journey to the hospital,
the soldiers they had struggled so hard to save would die.
The winter cold made everything more difficult.

Mairi and Elsie thought long and hard about what they
could do. There had to be a better way to save lives.
They hated to see the men suffer on the bumpy road to Furnes.
Clearly, the only answer was for Mairi and Elsie to move
closer to the fighting. That way they could treat the wounded
soldiers quickly, and help them recover enough to travel on to
hospital. It would put the two women in much greater danger,
but their minds were made up.

There was a small village called Pervyse right next to enemy lines. Most of the houses had been bombed and stood empty, with shattered windows and roofs open to the sky. A large area of flooded farmland 13 kilometres long and eight kilometres wide stretched between the village and the enemy guns. This was thanks to the Belgian army, who had opened the sluice gates on the River Yser near the sea at Nieuport. The shallow lake they created held the German invaders back, as no troops or heavy machinery could get across the wide stretch of waist-deep water. It was too shallow for boats and too deep and muddy for men on foot.

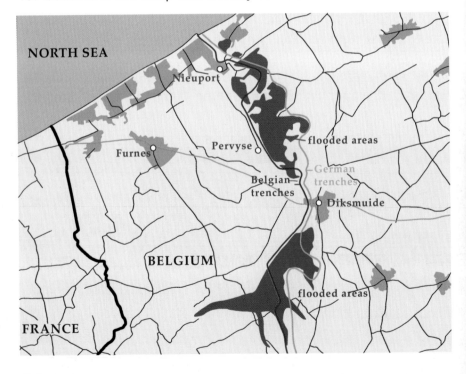

Although the houses in Pervyse were in ruins, a few of them had an underground cellar that could be used as a shelter. Mairi and Elsie proposed their idea to Dr Munro. They could set up a first-aid station in a cellar, and provide early treatment to wounded soldiers on the front lines. Once they were strong enough, the men could be driven to the hospital at Furnes. This would solve the problem of so many dying of shock on the journey.

the village of Pervyse

Dr Munro was not convinced. He felt it was far too dangerous for two women to work so close to the fighting. Elsie argued that it was the only way forward. The soldiers had to be treated in the first few hours or they would be lost. Mairi agreed. In her view, they only needed an extra day or so to get the wounded men ready to travel. Both Mairi and Elsie felt strongly that they should try everything they could to save lives.

Dr Munro could see that the two nurses were determined. He agreed to let one of the other ambulance drivers take a car and go with them, but that was all the help he could offer. They would have to leave the Flying Ambulance Corps and set up on their own. Mairi and Elsie would have to find money for food, petrol and medical supplies themselves. Did that put them off? Not one bit.

8 THE MOVE TO PERVYSE

On 22nd November, Mairi and Elsie set
up their British First Aid Post in a cellar
house in Pervyse. The space was about three
metres by four, with a low ceiling and only
the dim light from grates in the pavement
above. To furnish it, Mairi and Elsie had to
scavenge what they could find from other
bombed-out houses in the village. The first
thing they needed was a stove for heating
and cooking.

Two Belgian soldiers helped them gather
a table and some chairs as well. They built
a bed by laying straw on the floor, held in by
a wooden frame. Mairi explored a nearby
farmhouse and found plates, knives, forks
and spoons. She also brought back a big
copper pot for cooking. They made soup from
the cabbages, turnips and potatoes they dug
up from village gardens and nearby fields.

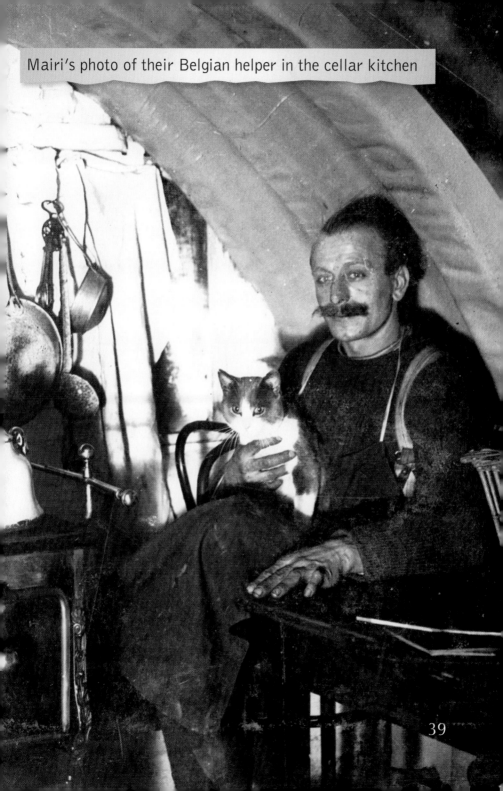

Mairi's photo of their Belgian helper in the cellar kitchen

Soon they had a collection of pets too! Three stray cats moved into the warm shelter, and a little black-and-white terrier joined them. They were good company, and kept the rats away. For a while, they even had a fox living in the garden!

Elsie, Mairi and their Belgian helper with all the pets

Elsie grew very fond of the terrier and named him Shot. Mairi loved the cats, and was given a new kitten for her birthday by an English officer. In time, they added a few chickens who earned their keep by laying eggs.

As well as providing nursing care for wounded soldiers, the First Aid Post served as a soup kitchen for all the men stationed nearby. Early every morning, Mairi and Elsie took hot soup to the men shivering in the frozen trenches. During the day, a big pot of hot chocolate was always simmering on the stove. Mairi and Elsie filled the mugs of all the soldiers who crowded around during breaks in the fighting. In the evening, they took hot chocolate to the trenches to keep the soldiers warm. When they could, they also gave out woollen socks, scarves, sweets, biscuits, soap and writing paper that had been donated.

Word spread quickly that two British nurses were providing care and support to the Belgian troops at the front.

Mairi and Elsie in a trench with Belgian soldiers

Mairi and Elsie were the only nurses for miles around because it was so dangerous. The soldiers called them the "Angels of Pervyse".

9 FUNDRAISING AND FAME

As time passed, Mairi and Elsie became famous back home. War correspondents and photographers came to visit them, and then published articles in newspapers and magazines across Europe. Soon everyone in Britain had read about the "British Nurses Who Risk Their Lives" and "English Women Under Fire". They were celebrated as heroines, and their faces appeared so often on magazine covers that they became celebrities. Lots of important people wanted to meet them, including top military commanders, politicians, rich donors and even royalty! The King and Queen of Belgium visited several times and awarded Mairi and Elsie medals for bravery.

Running the First Aid Post in Pervyse cost money, and Mairi and Elsie had to travel back to Britain whenever they could to raise more funds. Thanks to all the publicity in magazines and newspapers, Mairi and Elsie were greeted by large crowds on their visits home. Everyone knew what they were doing and wanted to help. They gave talks about their work in town halls and hotels up and down the country. Elsie was very good at describing the terrible dangers and difficulties they faced. She explained how important it was to treat the soldiers quickly to save more lives. Mairi called for donations of socks, bandages, pillows and blankets. On every stop of their fundraising tour, the money poured in. Wealthy donors even gave them ambulances and cars to take back with them!

Mairi's former headmistress, Jessie Wight, thought Mairi was a true inspiration for the school. She invited Mairi to speak to the pupils, and set up the Chisholm Fund to raise money for her.

A popular English actress named Eva Moore was also inspired by Mairi and Elsie. She wrote letters to all the big magazine editors asking them to support the Heroines of Pervyse. She also appealed directly to her fans. At the end of her performances on stage, she would stop the applause and ask the audience to donate money for Mairi and Elsie's war work. In London, Eva Moore organised fundraising gala events at the Alhambra Theatre with lots of other famous actors and singers. With 4,000 people in the audience, the donations were amazing!

Eva Moore and her husband

10 THE END OF THE WAR

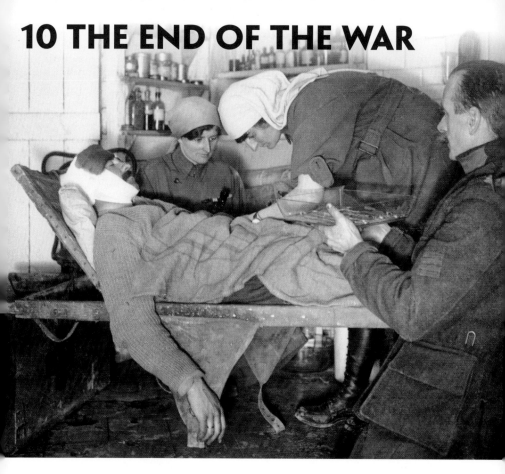

Once they had enough money and supplies to keep the First Aid Post running, Mairi and Elsie went back to Pervyse. In all, they spent nearly four years there, sleeping on straw fully clothed, washing once a week with a bucket, and eating tinned tomatoes, sardines and salt-cured beef. They worked day and night to save lives, risking their own as bombs rained down and bullets flew around them.

In the final year of the war, they were nearly killed themselves. A dry spring in 1918 meant that the floodwaters that had kept the Germans back for over three years began to recede.

In March, heavy bombing started over Pervyse and Nieuport, lasting for two weeks. It got so bad that Mairi and Elsie had to take cover in a dugout behind the cellar house. Suddenly, a **mustard gas shell** smashed into the dugout, and poisonous gas filled the passage. Shot the terrier barked a warning, and Mairi and Elsie rushed to put on their gas masks. The three cats hid under a blanket and survived, but the brave dog did not. Mairi and Elsie were badly affected by the gas, and were taken to hospital.

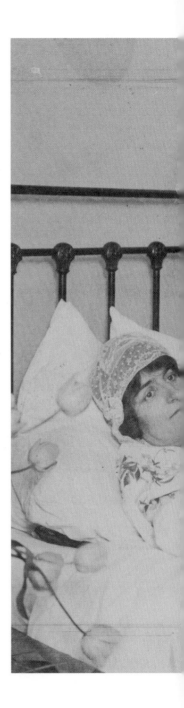

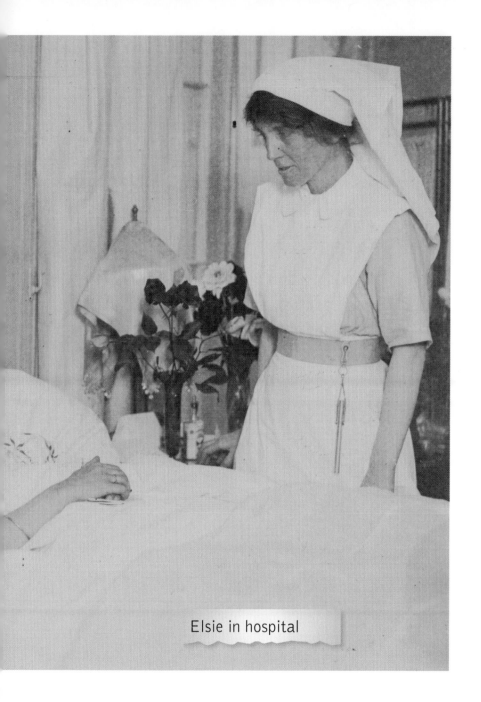

Elsie in hospital

By the time they recovered from their injuries, the war was nearly over. The First Aid Post was closed and Mairi took the three cats home to England. When they were well enough to work again, Mairi and Elsie still wanted to help. They joined the newly formed Women's Royal Air Force in London to work as drivers and mechanics in the final six months of the war. They continued to appear in public to raise funds for war hospital supplies and ambulances.

Mairi and Elsie were famous, but once the war was over, they had to start new lives. After all they had been through, it's hard to believe that Mairi was only 22 years old!

People in London celebrate the end of the war

11 AFTER THE WAR

As the years passed, Mairi's health suffered because of her war injuries. In 1921, aged 25, she moved to Scotland to raise ducks and chickens. By the time she was 30, she'd won all sorts of prizes for her birds. Whatever Mairi turned her hand to, she was a champion!

Today, there is a bronze sculpture of Mairi Chisholm and Elsie Knocker in the town of Ypres in Belgium. It was unveiled on 22nd November 2014, exactly 100 years after the cellar-house in Pervyse was opened. The sculpture celebrates two amazing women whose courage and kindness saved thousands of lives. They truly were the Angels of Pervyse.

GLOSSARY

the Channel the narrow stretch of sea between England and France

dispatch riders motorcycle riders hired by the British military to carry messages between headquarters and military units

"Flying" Ambulance Corps a group of British volunteers gathered by Dr Hector Munro to drive ambulances and transport wounded soldiers to field hospitals near the fighting in Belgium

music hall a popular form of theatre in Victorian and Edwardian Britain (1850–1918)

mustard gas shell a bomb containing a chemical that blistered the skin and the lungs; this gas was widely used by Germany against enemy forces from July 1917

refugees people caught up in war who travel to other countries seeking safety

shell shock a serious nervous reaction caused by repeated life-threatening explosions of bombs (shells); many soldiers suffered mental breakdowns due to stress during the First World War

sidecar a metal capsule attached to the side of a motorcycle with one outside wheel, for carrying a passenger

snipers soldiers who shoot from a distance using long-range weapons

trenches long, narrow ditches lined with sandbags from which soldiers shot at the enemy (who were hiding in their own trenches)

Women's Emergency Corps a group founded in 1914 to train female doctors, nurses and motorcycle messengers to help in the war effort

MAIRI'S JOURNEY

ENGLAND

August 1914: Mairi and Elsie ride to London to join the Women's Emergency Corps

London

Whin Croft, Dorset

Autumn 1913: Mairi gets her first motorbike and meets Elsie

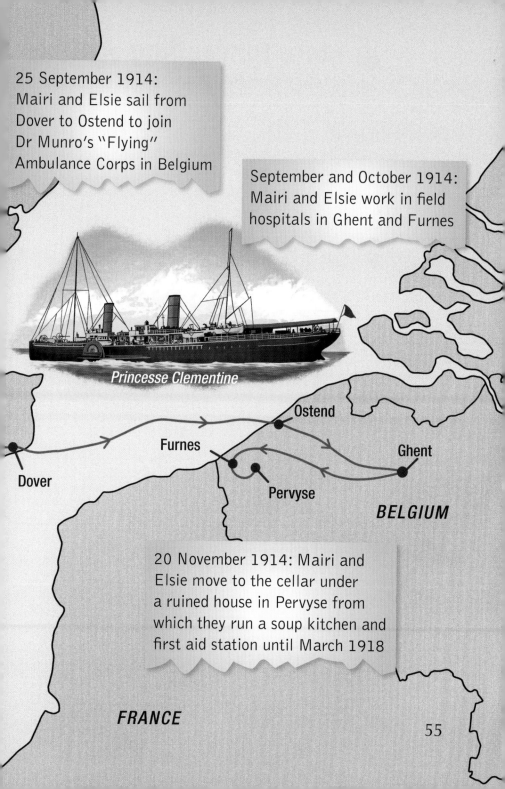

25 September 1914:
Mairi and Elsie sail from
Dover to Ostend to join
Dr Munro's "Flying"
Ambulance Corps in Belgium

September and October 1914:
Mairi and Elsie work in field
hospitals in Ghent and Furnes

Princesse Clementine

Ostend

Furnes

Ghent

Dover

Pervyse

BELGIUM

20 November 1914: Mairi and
Elsie move to the cellar under
a ruined house in Pervyse from
which they run a soup kitchen and
first aid station until March 1918

FRANCE

55

Ideas for reading

Written by Gill Matthews
Primary Literacy Consultant

Reading objectives:
- summarise the main ideas drawn from more than one paragraph, identifying key details that support the main ideas
- retrieve, record and present information from non-fiction
- provide reasoned justification for their views

Spoken language objectives:
- articulate and justify answers, arguments and opinions
- use spoken language to develop understanding through speculating, hypothesising, imagining and exploring ideas

Curriculum links: History – A study of an aspect or theme in British history that extends pupils' chronological knowledge beyond 1066

Interest words: summary, rejection, ultimatum

Resources: ICT, relevant non-fiction books

Build a context for reading
- Give children a few minutes to explore the cover of the book. Discuss what kind of book this is and what they would expect to find in it.
- Establish what children know about biographies.
- Focus on the back-cover blurb and explore what children know about the First World War.

Understand and apply reading strategies
- Read pp2–9 aloud to the children. Explore how they feel about Mairi being a mechanic and riding a motorbike. Check they understand that it would have been very unusual at the beginning of the 20th century. Discuss what kind of person Mairi might have been.
- Demonstrate how to briefly summarise Chapter 1.
- Allocate one chapter from Chapters 2 to 7 to each child. Ask them to read their chapter and to develop a brief summary of it. Take feedback in numerical order so that each child knows what has happened in the biography. Repeat this process with chapters 8 to 11.